A Novel by K. Larsen

LYING IN WAIT
Copyright © 2015 by K. Larsen
Second Edition

A Novel by <u>K. Larsen</u>
Cover by: <u>Cover Me Darling</u>
Editing: E. Adams

Other K. Larsen Books

30 Days ~ FREE

Committed

Bloodlines Series

All can be read as stand-alone books.

Tug of War ~ FREE

Objective

Resistance

Target 84

Stand Alones

Dating Delaney

Saving Caroline

Prologue

*O*pen.

She struggled to force her eyes open.

Agony.

Please. Please.

She waited for the white-hot agony to pass.

She was exhausted. Tired. So tired.

Her eyes snapped open finally.

Unfocused.

Yes, that's it.

The world was bleary. She blinked.

Still hazy. Unfocused.

Stay with me.

How?

Unconscious. For how long, she did not know.

Her eyelids felt as if cinder blocks sat atop them.

They dropped, closed. It was too hard to fight it.

She dreamed voices.

Rest. Just rest. You're safe. You're safe now fiore mio.

Matteo.

Safe.

Blackness.

Chapter 1

March 2014

~ Matteo ~

~***~

LYING IN WAIT- To constitute murder by lying in wait there must be an intentional infliction upon the person killed of bodily harm involving a high degree of probability that it will result in death and which shows a wanton disregard for human life.

~***~

As far as Matteo was concerned, Gabriel Fontaine had sealed his fate the day he pulled the proverbial trigger and left his wife for dead in Paris. Matteo had witnessed it and in doing so, had evolved. He'd been concealed a safe distance from her. He watched in terror as Gabriel pulled her into an embrace. In horror as he'd pulled a knife and plunged it into her back. What a coward he'd been. A cruel coward. In that one instant, he'd gone from doting best friend who dutifully stepped aside, who tucked his feelings for Celeste away because she'd been elated and he wanted nothing more than her happiness, to a man who would take what he wanted. And he'd wanted Celeste. He knew he should have run, gotten as far away from her as he could. Far away from the violence that surrounded her. But he couldn't do it.

He knew it was selfish but if he lost her, it would destroy him. So he'd changed right alongside her. Let the shadows and memories consume him over the years.

He sat near the window in their rental wondering, worrying really, about his wife.

Wife. Such a boring word. It did nothing to describe their connection. The depth of it. The meaning of it. They were more . . . intricate. He lit a cigarette. Inhaled. Exhaled. Chuckled to himself. She secretly loved the odor but she would be nagging him if she were here. But she wasn't. So he enjoyed his smoke earnestly.

Matteo wouldn't be able to see her for another week. He worried she wouldn't be able to go through with it in the end. That she would grow too fond of the girl. Celeste had a soft spot for people. She was never able to give in fully to the fury that fueled her. But now she wore her hatred like a neon sign. Easy to read. He watched the sky fade from pink to navy. They had come so far together.

As he did most evenings over the past week, he reached for her journal. The leather bound book was now scratched and supple from years of use. He stubbed out his cigarette, leaned back into the oversized chair, and flipped it open to the first page. It wasn't an invasion of her privacy. She knew he read it. He simply liked to see her handwriting. To read her thoughts. To hear her voice in his mind. She'd left him the journal for safe keeping while she was away. Said to read it if he wanted. It was their story.

A love story.

He flipped to the beginning. *Gabriel.* The name still left a sour taste on his tongue and a burn in his chest. Soon enough the man would be decimated. His life a sad pile of rubble. He didn't want to read the hopeless, empty words from the very beginning, so he skipped a couple entries in.

~***~

1994 - June

My mother used to soak in a lavender, eucalyptus and salt bath every night with a too-full glass of chardonnay. She'd sag in the tub and let the aromatic bath salts whisk away her non-existent stress. The scent of lavender now burns my nostrils. The sachets Matteo put in my bureau drawer were meant to be a kind gesture. Soothing. He couldn't have known that particular scent would irritate me and I hadn't been able to tell him. It was a week before I could rightfully form a sentence out loud. Each time I spoke it came out a sob. A lump of heartbreak. It came out as agony.

I can't do anything about it though. I'm dependent on Matteo for everything. I can't get up. I'm trapped in this bed. Tubes vining around me – from me. I'm stifled. Restless. Hungry. The blinding pain is nothing compared to the scope of my heartbreak. Gabriel left me for dead. My own husband. It was all a farce – our marriage, our love. Well, for him anyways. For me, I was just the naive woman who didn't know. The woman who blindly loved her husband. The one who didn't suspect a damn thing until it was far too late. The television repeats the same sad stories with no updates on the missing woman.

Me.

They show a sorrowful looking Gabriel. My parents. Esteemed Biochemist's Wife Gone Without a Trace. No leads in the Celeste Fontaine disappearance; family distraught. Yes. He's a great actor. My parents must be terrified. They should be. They're stuck grieving with a wolf. A wolf who stabbed me in the back, literally.

So I've taken to writing. Matteo brought me a

beautiful leather-bound journal. Endless pages of blank space to fill. I sit here and write. In an attempt to make sense of it, to see it clearly, I'm getting it all down. The scratching of my pen on paper like someone murmuring to me from far away. From underwater. The old me, telling a tale. History shared. I've decided that it will be cathartic. That it will be my therapy.

My stitches itch. The scar on my back won't ever be pretty. Matteo did his best to stich me up – and thank God he did - but the collapsed lung made his rescue a little more intense. I can't remember much. Just hitting the pavement. The sound of Gabriel's shoes slapping the ground as he walked away and left me there. Knowing I wanted to scream. Knowing I was supposed to because somewhere Matteo was waiting for me. And knowing I couldn't. I couldn't get a damned sound out.

Matteo.

That man. He didn't need me to scream. He was there, waiting. He came. He saved me from death. God those first few weeks were a nightmare. How he managed to move me to safety and save me I will never fully understand. He calls it adrenaline. I call it heroic. His veterinary training was invaluable given the state I was left in. Albeit animals are a different game, he managed to perform surgery on me, and save my life.

The day before Gabriel came to me under the Eiffel Tower Matteo and I had set up a safe house. Just as a precaution really. We thought we were so clever. I don't think either of us truly anticipated using it. We surely would have chosen better had we known.

~***~

Matteo thought back to those days. The days before the two of them evolved. He could scarcely believe the situation that had presented itself before them. He'd known Celeste for decades and it nearly brought him to his knees right alongside her when they'd discovered the truth. His relationship with Dr. B had taught him to be careful when it came to government agencies and his learned distrust had been their saving grace in the end.

~***~

1994 – July

*O*ur studio flat is in the heart of Paris. Right under everyone's noses—four weeks now. I exist. Sometimes it makes me laugh. I'm right here! I want to scream, shout it out. But I can't. We are just three blocks from FogPharm. From Gabriel's lab. From Monique. Obviously she hasn't been in the news. Gabriel's a smart man. He's playing it smart right now . . . but everything has only just begun.

~***~

What torture those days had been. How hard it had been while she lay there unconscious. In serious condition, it had been hard to think past her in that room, to listen to anything more than the steady beep of her heart monitor. Matteo had burned both ends of the candle. Working still, playing the grief-stricken friend, keeping up appearances and listening diligently for any clues Gabriel might emit that would aid him in keeping Celeste safe. His heart had constricted with pain each time he and Celeste sat and watched the news. At her face, her horror, as she had listened and watched her insidious husband spew lies to reporters, to her parents. It had been the only way though. He couldn't shelter her from the situation. If they were going to survive, and more importantly move on, she had to face it head on.

~***~

1994 - *July*

My heart is a lesion. Throbbing. A rotting organ. An open wound. I'm angry still. Furious really. That fury, it's a seed, small and inconsequential but I can feel it has taken root. It's growing. It makes me wonder what it will look like tomorrow, the day after. The knife in my heart plunges deeper and deeper.

I have trouble sleeping, and it's not just the pain now, it's the nightmares. My nightmares are frequent. Most always the same. Gabriel coming for me. When he reaches me, I can't scream. I try — I suck the air into my lungs and I propel it out — but there's no sound, just a rasping. Sometimes, in my nightmares, I find myself smiling up at him. Grisly and pale. Pleading with my eyes for him to see the hurt that I harbor. To see the state I'm in. To feel something about it.

Matteo sits night after night in a ridiculous yellow armchair at the foot of my bed. The tubes prevent him from sleeping with me. I've told him to go home so many times it's become a joke. Dressings need to be changed. Drainage bags emptied. He refuses to make me spend a night alone. He is the light in my darkness. My sanity. I feel like I'm going mad trying to make sense of my life. Trying to look back and decipher what were truths and what weren't. There is no greater agony, nothing more tormenting than not knowing, which for me, will never stop. I will never know the extent of Gabriel's betrayal. I will never know if any of our moments together were pure. They could have all been a lie, and it's likely they were.

I'm so cold inside. Gabriel's betrayal cut me down to the bone. I imagine him dancing all over my soul in my dreams. Last night there was a thunder storm filled with cracks of thunder, a surge of lightning. I jackknifed upright. I gritted my teeth against the pain in my ribs. Matteo leapt from his seat. Rubbed my back. Whispered I'm safe. It was a dream. Something important had happened in my dream. I kept trying to to hold on to it, but the more I tried, the further it disappeared. When I finally closed my eyes again, my head was filled with images of vicious deception. With the things I wanted, the things I thought I had and the lies they all turned out to be. What a joke.

I would never tell Teo, but I like the smell of his

cigarette smoke. I used to have one with him, when we were young and out drinking now and again. It's arousing to me, that smell; it reminds me of him only. He's cut himself shaving today, there's blood on his cheek covered with a tiny piece of toilet paper stuck to it. His hair is damp and he smells like soap and aftershave. It's silly writing about him while he's six feet from me but our bodies are so close here in this tiny studio, I can smell his scent, clean in this dingy room, strong and astringent. Safe. Sound. Comforting.

~***~

Those days had been the worst for him. Bearing witness to her depression, her heartache, her desire for answers. Even still, Cece carried herself with grace. It hung from her shoulders always. Matteo pushed up from the chair and walked to the kitchen. He stretched. Filled a kettle and set it on the burner. After fixing himself a mug of tea he worked his way back into the living room, back to his chair. The house was quiet. Too quiet without his love there. He would have to be patient. This game was working its way to completion and once it was over they would be truly whole. Able to live in the light, no shadows in their hearts. He hadn't known how to comfort her, how to ease her pain then. He'd never seen Celeste so conflicted. Her wounds had still been fresh, and then the anger that had been simmering in her blood finally began to seep out.

~***~

1994 - September

"Celeste Fontaine Still Missing". I've been gone more than three months now, and the story has become sensational news. Light slips through the slats on the blind. When the studio window is cracked open, I can taste the carbon monoxide rising from the street below. I hate this place.

Monique is showing. Really showing. She stood between Gabriel, wearing my parents' company lab coat, and my parents in the latest press conference. The ache in my chest is almost unbearable. Maybe that was the moment when things started to go wrong for Gabriel and me, the moment he began to see us not only as couple but as a potential family, complete with children. I couldn't have them, and after that just the two of us would never be enough for him. I'm distracted. I don't want to see her face, her protruding belly, her nearness to him. They called her a friend of the missing. She was not my friend.

Matteo visited my parents two days ago after visiting Dr. B's lawyer to pick up the last of his signed estate documents. I was safe. Before I had gone to my house for the last time I had signed all the necessary paperwork for my inheritance from Dr. B. From my grandfather. Free and clear. I can be missing now and it's okay because it's all set up and waiting. I can be dead and I made it all mine. To disappear with. I made it Matteo's. Everything.

My parents grumbled to Matteo that Gabriel was acting strange. Nervous. That he was talking of resigning from his position. Matteo played along and told them the pressure of my disappearance probably was too much for him. Lies. This studio I'm stuck in, we're stuck in, is bare essentials. It's got a layer of filth that no matter how hard Matteo scrubs doesn't come off. It would take a grenade to clean this prison. There is one small window. He put the bed (and me) right near it, but it doesn't help my feeling cooped up.

Some say that joy is greater than sorrow, and others say sorrow is greater; I say they are inextricable. When one sits with you, the other is simply asleep within you. Sometimes I pity myself. Memories jolt me painfully. They swaddle me as I cry. I despise the power that lies in those wet drops that fall from my eyes. When that sadness surfaces in front of me, larger than any I have witnessed before, I realize that something is happening to me. That life has not forgotten me. That it holds me in its hand and will not let me fall. Learning to live is learning to let go. Unanswered questions are a part of life. Strange, that all that is now magnified and colossal at the same time, all that was, now isn't. Perhaps gradually, someday far in the future, I will, without even noticing it, be content. Be open. Memories can tell me only what I once was. They cannot help me find what I must become.

I wonder what Matteo would do if I turned to face him and kissed his mouth. I watch him often. The way he looks at me. The way his lips move when he speaks. His gentleness with me. His devotion. There is a tension growing between us. Intensity. It's sublime torture. The way he looks at me. The way he's patient with me.

~***~

In hindsight, that had been the start of their union. Their friendship long established, those early days in hiding, in healing, had sparked something inside her. Something that wasn't innocent or friendly. It was the start of furtive glances stolen, smiles that promised something more, innocent touches that burned brighter than a supernova. The tension that kept rising, and the undeniable attraction grew more tender with each day that passed. He hadn't known then of course, but reading her words took him back to a moment he'd long forgotten.

He'd cancelled his appointments for the day effectively calling in sick. Pushing through the studio door he surprised Celeste. Startled by the unexpected visit she let out a small puff of air that set Max on high alert at the end of her bed. The dog lay back down quickly.

"What are you doing here?" she asked wearing a grin. She lazily pet the dog. He sauntered to the kitchenette and set down a paper bag. He poked through the cabinet until he found a suitable cup for the flowers under his arm.

"I wanted to spend the day with you. I know you're bored." Setting the flowers into the water-filled cup he

carried them to her nightstand and set them there.

"Did I do something to deserve your company?" she laughed before admiring the bouquet.

"No. A man can miss a woman can't he?" He was nervous. His statement was more suggestive than friendly and he wasn't sure how it would be received. He'd long been in love with Celeste. Since the class they'd met in so many years ago. She regarded him with a half-smile and nodded. Pulling a paperback from the paper bag he tossed it onto the bed. He watched as she reached toward her feet to retrieve the book. Picking up his own novel and a bunch of grapes he made his way back to where she lay. She scooted, as best she could to the left, allowing more room for him to sit comfortably next to her. Their shoulders brushed together.

He sat, book open in his lap, watching her read. Watching the way her expression changed each time she read a scene. The way she popped grapes into her mouth. Her lips. The way the hair on his arm stood up with a static-like feeling each time their arms brushed each other's. There was a tension between them that never used to be. Every so often he'd catch her watching him and vice versa. Stolen moments that seemed to drive the temperature in the small space up and up until combustion was inevitable.

Still healing, Celeste grew tired easily. As she drifted off, he played with a strand of her hair. If she only knew how much she played with his emotions. What would it finally be like to kiss her? To feel her lips on his. Those two soft pink lips. He sometimes caught her looking at him with want. But that couldn't be. Not now. Not so close on the heels of her husband. The mere thought of Gabriel ignited something deep inside him that had never existed before. Hate. It ran deep too. Watching Gabriel pull her into his arms that day. Watching the knife come out. Knowing she couldn't see it. He'd been blind with rage. With a fury so explosive that he'd almost fucked their entire plan by showing himself. Never before had he needed to use such great restraint. But he had. He'd seen the truth behind all of Gabriel's lies in that moment. And now, now she was here, safe for now, alive. He watched her snore lightly and smiled at her. He would do, had done, anything for her even if his feelings were never returned.

Matteo set the journal aside and cracked his neck. He'd been in his wife's life for the better part of four decades. Their story was a difficult one; not always, but enough so that he was certain that they would make it through anything if they were together. He'd sacrificed much for her but ultimately, if he could go back and change anything, he wouldn't.

Not everyone would understand their connection. Their mutual desire for resolution. It bonded them further. It was unique to them and he coveted it. It was also nearing its end. They had worked, watched and sat idle for years upon years and now they were winding up for their grand slam, where the game would be won and then what? They had shared dreams, of travel, of relaxation, of seeing what the world had to offer to those blessed with the wealth to pay for it but a small part of him worried that it wouldn't be enough for her. That she would feel a letdown when this was all over.

He shook the thoughts from his head and stood, stretched his back, hearing the gratifying pop of vertebrae. It was late and he needed rest. Tomorrow he needed to visit a few nurseries. Shop plants. It had to be just the right one.

~***~

Matteo's day was rather bland. He'd purchased a potted Gloxinia plant for his wife. Dropped it at the rental then left to follow Tad around for a few hours. The tennis pro was a bore. His tan was fake, his gleaming white teeth displayed an obnoxious glare and the way he not-so-discreetly manhandled Monique was offensive. He'd rather be home reading, watching terrible daytime TV or really doing anything else. But this was a critical part of the plan and needed time invested into it. Monique had been seeing Tad for a good long while now. It was full blown love, easily readable in her expressions. Whether or not Tad truly returned that love, wasn't as obvious. No matter. All that was needed were Monique's feelings. It would truly be a shame the day she got his suicide letter insinuating she was the cause. She was mentally frail since losing her son; it was as obvious as the sun shining. So frail that it would only take one more small intrusion to break her.

He thought about Cece, how she looked like an angel in the bright summer sun. The way the glassy blue water seemed to wink at her on clear days. So full of grace that when she walked, she floated like a feather. So special. His.

Monique turned in Tad's arms outside the hotel. Kissed him passionately. When they tore themselves apart Matteo could practically see the thorn twist in her side. There was hope in their eyes, as if they were thinking that through the storm they would reach the shore together. But Monique would be landing on the shore alone. Matteo smiled. His hands were tied, for now. But the longer she gave herself away to Tad, the more effective the revenge.

Chapter 2

April 2014

~ Matteo ~

~***~

LYING IN WAIT- waiting and watching for an opportune time to act. The lying in wait need not continue for any particular period of time provided that its duration is such as to show a state of mind equivalent to premeditation or deliberation.

~***~

He could hear it in her voice as she talked about the girl and it made him nervous. Celeste seemed almost giddy when she relayed their first few visits. *What a brat she is, Matteo. I think she likes me. She's got something broken in her. It's evident in her eyes. I can use this. I can use this to build a relationship with her, to gain her trust.* It was beyond him why she cared about gaining Annabelle's trust. Being at the assisted living facility was just a cover, a means to an end. She didn't need to stay longer than necessary but as their visit progressed, Celeste made it clear that she intended on staying till the end of Annabelle's sentence. That the plan had changed. She was telling Annabelle the story of her. Of them. It was dangerous and he said as much but Cece wouldn't be swayed. Doubts were dangerous. Matteo sighed and smiled at his wife. She was a force to be reckoned with and he knew that no matter how much he wanted this to play out quickly she was now bent on making this last piece of revenge personal. Very personal. He leaned in and kissed her forehead.

"I know Teo. I know," she sighed. "This wasn't the plan."

"No, but if it is what you need, I will wait." Cece looked up at him and grinned. She grabbed his face and pulled him to her. The kiss fiery and passionate. He kissed her back forcefully, truthfully, ardently.

"You are my moon Teo." He pushed her soft hair over her shoulder.

"And you are my tide fiore mio." She rested her cheek on his chest.

"You smell delicious. I miss this smell. Cigarettes and soap."

He smirked. "I miss you. How can I possibly survive for six months only seeing you twice a month?" He sounded weak but it was also the truth, and they were always honest with each other. Over the last twenty years there had been only a handful of times they had been apart more than a few days. This would test them, challenge them, but he knew deep in his soul they would survive. They had to.

"This gloxinia is gorgeous. I'll think of you every time I look at it," she commented.

"I know love, that's exactly why I brought it."

"You jealous? How unlike you," she laughed. He smoothed his thumb over the apple of her cheek.

"Jealous of the other residents? No fiore mio, jealousy has nothing to do with it. My motive is selfish. I want you thinking of me, of us, of our future, while you're here."

"Teo, Teo, Teo. You're worried."

He was. And he knew Cece could read him without effort. Why he tried concealing anything from the woman was unknown. "Sì, Celeste. You aren't as ruthless as you want to believe. And that's okay. It's why I love you. I don't want you to grow to like the girl-"

"Annabelle," she cut him off. He sighed and ran a hand through his cropped hair.

"Yes, like *her*. Gabriel's daughter," he amended.

Celeste's eyes held his. A moment passed between them. He knew that she heard him. That she understood his concerns just from a look.

"I won't get too close my love. I'm doing this for us. You are my future. We're so close now to having our lives back free and clear," she said.

"Yes. We are."

Celeste pushed up to her toes and snaked her arms around his neck. He bent slightly and scooped her up, hands holding her very tight, very perfect rear. "Enough talk of things we already know. Give me something to dream about until I see you again, husband," she cooed. Matteo carried her to the bed and reverently stripped his wife bare while placing lingering kisses as he exposed each new section of golden, cashmere-soft skin. "Anything you want fiore mio." With the ghost of his lips still on her skin, he rid himself of his clothes and worshipped the body that belonged to the woman he loved so deeply.

As he pulled in the driveway of his temporary home he felt lighter. His visit with Cece renewed his focus. He climbed out of the car, swinging the door shut behind him. He held on tight to the memory of the feel of her hair sliding through his fingers, of her lips, soft against his skin. The strength he drew from her in the harshest times kept him hard and attached to the truth of what they were doing. Murder. Utter destruction. His softer side had bled out watching Cece lying on the cold hard pavement. It had vanished as he watched Gabriel put a knife in her back and walk away without a glance backward. He rubbed the bridge of his nose hard, as if he could rub out those memories, the sting of them, away.

~***~

1996 - Paris/Spain

Matteo says it's not safe here anymore. That we need to leave Paris now. It's becoming too hard for him to keep up appearances and I'm restless and cooped up. The last year and change has been a sacrifice but it seems there is no longer anything to gain by being here. We've learned nothing new in months and this one room studio driving me mad. Sometimes I think it killed Max. Even the dog couldn't take it.

I was.

I was.

I was.

Sometimes the weariness of a massive stone wall spanning the banks of endless ocean hangs in my soul. Other times I am as numb as the morning fog that dances on the ocean's edge. A change is taking place within my soul. It's difficult to adapt because I'm no longer that old person, but not yet the new. In the rising of the sun and in its setting I remember her, my old self. In the introduction of buds and the rebirth of spring I remember her. When I'm lost and sick at heart, I remember her. Every time I think of myself, of who I am . . . it's based on who I was. I feel adrift. I was hopeful. I was kind. I was content, vivacious, the color yellow. Now I don't know. I've been stripped of all the characteristics I associated with myself. I'm dark brown, like mud. I'm confused, anxious, furious and vengeful. I'm split. Torn between two sides of myself that battle for the limelight. Like an index finger on the trigger of a loaded gun, I can feel the temperature inside me rising. I'm coming into my own again. But I'm halfway to hell; I've made my bed.

I gave so much heart that I am now heartless. I need to fill the empty void that is left over. There was darkness - so much darkness. Gabriel stole my soul for personal gain. He thinks he's something but consists of only money and opinions. I've been black inside. But that black has morphed into diamonds under all the pressure. That's exactly why I plot and watch and wait. Teo and I bought a one-way train ticket to Spain and I see that I am not afraid. Not really. I deserve this life for all the sacrifice I've made.

Maybe I'm crazy. Or foolish. Maybe I don't know how to love. But maybe I do. And I wonder, does it blow his mind that they never found my body? That I'm leaving him far behind. I wonder, does it stop his heart to know he's not my gravity anymore? His face is a work of art. His smile could light up the Eiffel Tower. But it's a shame that a man so handsome has such an ugly heart. Maybe he'll get married someday, and maybe she will worship him and maybe on his honeymoon he'll think of me. But it doesn't matter because I'm gone. It took the knife that pierced my lung to stab through the emotional walls that now lie in front of my heart.

The season of my grief evolves. I will not resist the tides. I will give into them. The waves will bring me back to shore. Teo is my moon guided by the tide. I believe in myself. I believe in Teo. I believe in our unlimited potential. I surrender. I surrender to my new self. To my new life.

~***~

Some questions Matteo asked himself at night were best left until morning. Some questions stuck up without warning, leaving him restless and anxious. *Be with me tonight, I'm lonely, cold.* He had thought. *Leave this crusade for vengeance.* But Cece was willing to be fearless and thus, he was too. The memory reminded his soul, so he would stay waiting for her. Gabriel destroyed everything Celeste thought was true and she wouldn't be satisfied-no they wouldn't be satisfied-until they had taken from him all his truths-his marriage, his children, his identity. Not too much longer now. They were growing ever closer. Visualizing it was so satisfying, pulling a cigarette out of the pack he kept in his breast pocket he tucked it between his lips before lighting it. Celeste fascinated him still. He flipped through pages of her journal. He had a constant distaste in his mouth when he thought of Gabriel. He closed his eyes for a moment, collecting himself. Letting his mind wander to a time that didn't revolve around *him.*

Them in the empty field in Canada with the stars, in the quaint cafes in Spain, at the restaurant where the course of her life-Dr. B's life, had changed, quiet candle lit dinners together, times spent in their bed talking about nothing and everything, their late night intimacy, the laughs they shared, the arguments, the make-up sex, the dancing, the kisses and arms tangled together. He missed the intoxicating scent of flowers in the air. Flowers she worked hard to cultivate. To grow. To nurture. Matteo wanted to find a strand of her hair tangled in the button of his shirt in the middle of the day, or hear the front door open and know by the lightness of her footsteps that she was home. He wanted to wake up to kisses from his love again.

He focused his attention, a small smile playing on his lips. *"Hearts bend because they can't break when they have true love to guide them through all that's thrown at them."* Cece had whispered that in his ear long ago in a remote house in Spain. It was true. It was their truth, together they could fair anything.

Chapter 3

May 2014

~ Matteo ~

*M*atteo hated that she wore the old locket. It seemed to be a part of her, to echo her heartbeat against her skin. It hung just above the swell of her breasts. It had no permission to hang there so close to her heart. It shone in the light from the window brilliantly. He gritted his teeth. His thoughts quickly turned stormy.

"Madison visited with Annabelle," Cece practically chirped. He lifted his gaze and ran fingers through her long hair, massaging her scalp. She shifted. Soft lips pressed to the hollow of his throat before she laid her head back on his chest. "Who is Madison?" he asked.

"Belle's best friend. She's not exactly what I would call a good choice in the friend department though. It seems their friendship is based on a rather superficial foundation."

"This is important why?" he asked.

"She told me about Brant." He felt a shudder run through her body. His hand drifted between them until it reached hers, their fingers linking. That day had been especially dark. Nothing could have prepared him for the disaster that she was after it had happened. He was supposed to be there with her for that task but in a fit of blind rage she'd gone from simply observing to acting. It was a burden he couldn't shoulder for her no matter how hard he tried.

"It destroyed her. Belle found him. All those questions we had. All those unanswered questions were laid bare for me."

Matteo hated sitting on the sidelines. Doing nothing but waiting while she took the brunt of this last leg of the journey.

"And . . ." he pushed.

"And although it wasn't meant to happen quite the way it did," she tilted her face upward to meet his eyes, "the result was exactly right."

"Cece."

"Teo, I'm fine. It was good to hear it - to get closure," she said. His eyes dropped to her mouth, that smile, those lips he wanted on him.

"How is it? Sitting with her, face to face? Building a relationship?"

Cece thought for a moment. "Odd. I try so hard to be distant but she's a bright girl you know. She's so lost in her life. Gabriel and Monique have truly done a number on her. Putting her down will actually put her out of her misery. It's almost a blessing," she smirked at him.

"I can do this for you. I would. You know that right?"

"Teo. I don't need you to. You've done so much. Loved so thoroughly. You are the light that keeps me sane."

"My hands are just as dirty as yours fiore mio," he countered earnestly.

"Your hands are as clean as I could keep them, and that is how I'd like them to stay. We are so close now. I want those hands to whisk me away when this is over – give me a real life. A meaningful life of marriage and love and days growing old happily together."

Matteo scoffed, mocking offense. "I've not done that thus far?"

She stretched her neck up and kissed him, biting his lip playfully. "You've done that and so much more."

He stilled. "My moon, kiss me like that again."

"My tide - forever."

He kissed her in the sensitive spot below her ear and heard her breath hitch. Rolling her onto her back he hovered over her. He took his time as he kissed her face, her neck, her throat, her clavicle, stopping only to look into her eyes.

~***~

Matteo sat in the kitchen at the table eating take-out. They'd only intended on being apart for a month, tops. Cece's change in plan was difficult for him. Six months felt never-ending. Through all the years they had lain in wait together. Planning meticulously how to go about everything and now he was alone, out of the loop most of the time while she was there with the Devil's daughter. He now had to rearrange his end of the plan as well. He had watched the man's comings and goings for months previously but now he had to find a new day and time to take him. He sighed and rubbed the backs of his hands over his eyes.

Matteo wanted to visit more but they'd both agreed it would be too dangerous. They needed to maintain as low a profile as possible, still. He couldn't be the man that people recognized visiting her daily. Infrequent was best, even if difficult.

Matteo trudged to the fridge, grabbed a beer and cracked it open. He retired to the living room for the remainder of the evening, leaving his dirty plate on the table for another time. Cece would chastise him for it if she were there. He flipped through the pages in her journal until he found the entries from 1996.

~***~

1996 - Spain

There was a memorial service for me. It's been so long now that no one holds out hope that I am coming back . . . or alive. Matteo went. Asked if anyone had contacted Mara. No one had, they couldn't find her current contact information. Gabriel didn't speak to him. Refused actually, so Matteo said. Made some sort of scene and left early. It struck me as odd until Matteo finished his tale. He drove by my old house. Gabriel's house. Monique was in the living room window. Holding an infant. Waving her free hand through the air clearly angry at something. Pain rips through me when I think of it. I don't want Teo to see me crying, to see me weak, so I keep my tears in.

That night in our adorable Spanish cottage Matteo lay in bed with me, traced my scar. It made me shiver. He asked my wishes, that I say out loud all my darkest desires. He promised no judgment. I talked of ripping apart Gabriel's life. Of being cunning and calculating and slowly stripping him of all he cherishes. Matteo asked how. To really dig deep, dive into the fantasy and get it all out. My tongue moved without thought, words tumbled from my mouth. Gabriel's career. Gabriel's child. Gabriel's relationship. All must go. All must be destroyed. A tense moment passed between us. Matteo stared so deeply into my soul that I thought for sure he could see the seed of fury that grows inside me. I thought for sure he would see the depths of hell reflected in my eyes. He kissed the tip of my nose. He smiled. He said 'How would you go about that?' and without hesitation I rattled off ideas. Suddenly, I feel like a newborn.

Vulnerable and exposed.

Covered in deceitful stickiness.

I fell asleep the next afternoon. When I woke, I was sweaty, panicky. Guilty. The constant push and pull of desire and restraint warring inside me. I want so badly to be able to hold on to it. Love is powerful. It can heal, it can lift - it can also drag you down into the depths of hell and burn you until you're no longer recognizable. So I must be careful with my heart.

And that next evening, I kissed Matteo.

I did it.

I was aching. Lingering in the past like a fool. I blew on the window and drew in the fog and this whole world opened up right before my eyes. Matteo made my life right, light. I took a leap. I stepped forward, closed the gap between our bodies, stood on tiptoe and kissed his lips. He didn't pull away from me.

His hands on my hips. My kiss on his lips. I didn't want the moment to end. And it struck me, I could do this for a long time - forever. His love, his commitment, it saved me. When I lost it, he held my hand. And he rushed to me and it set us free. He's my fault. My weakness. Is it a sin that I want Matteo so badly? My name on his lips, my sweat on his skin?

~***~

Night arrived shrouding the world in darkness. The moon had been the only light. He had seen the storm set in Cece's eyes. And right there curled up together as she spoke they tumbled and fell. Mountains had crumbled to the sea. The fighting was over. Through the storm they reached the shore, together. She didn't cry. Whatever made her happy, whatever she wanted he would provide. He vowed silently to be whatever Cece needed—whenever. Matteo remembered that day clearly. His memory needed no help to conjure the events that led to that halcyon moment.

She drew a broken heart in the fog on the window pane. There in the pouring rain and cold weather she just breathed against the glass. Matteo had trudged up the stairs, a bag of groceries under one arm, and seen the heart. He drew a question mark in the fog. She half-smiled through the cloudy window at him. He set the bag down under the small portico and exhaled a great breath against the glass. He drew a heart opposite her broken one. Then he drew a bridge between the two, from his side to hers. Right then he wanted to hold on to the feeling that coursed through him at her expression. He placed his bet on them, on Cece and himself. He picked up the bag and went inside. She watched him as he set the bag on the counter before approaching her.

"I'll be the one to cross over Cece. I'll come to you and we'll repair your heart together." His hand cupped her cheeks. He meant what he said. And right then, plain as day in her eyes, he knew his feelings for her were returned.

Their first kiss. Matteo recalled it vividly. That divine moment when all the walls came down. When their friendship blossomed into something he'd dreamed about for years. He had felt like he owned the world the moment his lips pressed against hers. There were no words to accurately describe what it felt like. What it made him feel. This woman, this friend knew his soul. She was his other half and he had always known it. He'd long ago been convinced that his only option to keep her in his life was to be happy for her and to be her friend. The torture of that reality had been excruciating. He'd watched passively as she dated Gabriel. As she said yes to his proposal. As she walked down the aisle to marry him. As she struggled, as she soared - he was there for it all, and it had been devastating. There were times he pushed her away, times he'd considered coming clean to profess his feelings but he hadn't. They were young. She came from a different lifestyle than he. There were other pressures of course and if she said no, he wouldn't have even had her friendship. No. He had never risked it.

Everything had changed when Dr. B died. When they discovered truths they weren't supposed to and in the end, when he'd saved her. He waited as she recovered. As she warred with herself, with her guilt, her fury and her heartbreak. And then, then he'd waited some more. The tension between them that first year together had grown to epic proportions. When those soft, supple lips he'd dreamed about met his he knew he'd never let them go back to anything less than lovers.

"You have no idea how many nights I've lain awake imagining this moment . . . what it would feel like to have you in my bed, my arms. I want your mouth on me, your hands on me. I want to taste you . . . savor you . . . devour you fiore mio. I've lusted. Longed."

Her eyes had darkened at his words. And in those next seconds she'd made his dreams come true. Cece had leapt into his arms, wrapping her legs and arms around him. Clung to him desperately. They couldn't get close enough.

They couldn't go fast enough. He'd let out a low groan, his kiss grew urgent and hungry. Her reciprocation, just as hungry. Any space between their bodies had been too much. They had been starved and had devoured each other time and time again that night. He'd whispered to her in Italian all the emotions he'd kept from her over the years. She'd cried and laughed and come so hard he was sure the windows were shattered from her scream.

It was after that he watched his soul-mate rise from the ashes of devastation and betrayal and become someone else. Someone he helped cultivate. For as much as he wanted Celeste, he wanted Gabriel to pay for the destruction and pain he'd caused. He stepped into Cece's hate-fire willingly, stoking the spark of revenge until a fire roared. It wasn't just Cece who changed - it had been him as well.

~***~

1996 - Spain

*M*y tears may be dried up now, but the heart never forgets. Just as entire forests burn to the ground and eventually grow anew, whatever I suffered, I kept on growing. There was a rip, a tear in the fabric of my life that won't ever be completely mended. But memories that let in *both the darkness of the Hell and the bright celestial light comfort me. I can let my pains bleed for a while yet still be open to the many joys in my life. I am grateful for the pain because I've learned from it.*

These emotions are beautiful, the weakness that comes after suffering. The deepened conviction that follows after grief, and the rousing to love again.

Anonymous packages began arriving at local news stations in France. Letters. Photographs. Details about the renowned biochemist Gabriel Fontaine. Stories started running on television and in the papers. Biochemist testing on human subjects. "Respected biochemist, Gabriel Fontaine working with CIA." "Infidelity afoot in unsolved biochemist's wife case."

It's funny to see my own words appear in the news. Gratifying really. I sat back and found myself smiling as week by week Gabriel made the papers. And wouldn't you know it . . . he's vanished. No one can find him. Consequently, no one can find Monique either. Shamed. Shunned. Embarrassed. I imagine they are all of those things now. I don't care where he's gone to. Not really. His career's been killed. Exposed. All those years and years of research for naught. I find myself smiling at the thought.

Delighted.

I've had dreams recently. I'm trapped in a room. Gabriel's voice on the other side of the door taunts me. But unlike my old dreams, in this one, when I look around, I'm in a nursery. There's a baby. Ssilky and new. I snatch it up in my arms and pull it close to my chest, to my heart. Monique's voice rings out over Gabriel's and when I look down, the infant doesn't belong to me. Shock rips through me. Suddenly the tiny infant's eyes turn black and cold. The longer I look at the baby, the less I feel, until I'm holding the baby out the window and letting go. And I'm laughing and careless as Gabriel and Monique's screams fill the space around me.

~***~

Matteo knew Cece would leave with every piece of Gabriel. He never underestimated the things that she would do. That they were doing. He took solace in knowing that in the depths of Gabriel's despair, the beast would think of them. Spring was cold and damp but soon the boiling heat of summer's awning would be upon them bringing the fiery temperatures of hell. Where Gabriel would rot.

~***~

1996 - Spain

Matteo and I married today!
It wasn't at all like my first wedding. It was so much better. Private, intimate, meant only to join two hearts. Shared only between two hearts. Months ago Matteo met a man while we had brunch a beautiful restaurant in town. They'd struck up easy conversation then. Over

the months he and Alarico formed a tight bond. And thank God for that. Alarico is a surprisingly well-connected man. Between him and the private investigator we hired to track Gabriel, we've managed to give ourselves new identities. Papers, IDs and all. It is because of this I was able to have the most splendid moment with Teo.

The sun shone down on us, heavenly in its glare, while the minister from the local church married us. I was impossible to ignore a man like my Teo. It was a crime against nature and I knew that with all of my heart. I am the luckiest woman alive. When the minister declared us Mr. and Mrs. Grant we'd shared a look and laughed heartily before he swept me up in a kiss that devoured my very soul. Jezebel and Ahab Grant. They were ludacris names, stolen from history.

It doesn't matter though; to each other we are Cece and Teo. The world outside us doesn't really exist. My Teo. My heart is so full. He sleeps so soundly next to me right now as I scribble this memory down. I am content. I am wrapped up in his love so wholly that everything else that eats at me disappears. It is divine.

~***~

Matteo closed the journal, a smile played on his lips. He retrieved a cigarette, lit it and enjoyed the sensation of smoke as it filled his lungs. Their life had been more than just Gabriel and revenge and plotting. Her entries in her journal had over the years become her outlet but the moments they'd shared away from those dark thoughts had been magic.

Their time in Spain had been spent dining, walking and dancing in the small town they resided in. They had long hot nights and lazy mornings. Just after their wedding he'd caught her flipping to a blank page in her journal and furiously scribbling on the page. He'd stilled her hand.

"Teo," she murmured, placing the pen in the crease of the journal and closing it. "Let me take this fury from you. Let me go and just take care of him, of her."

"You would lose everything, Teo," she'd said in a hoarse whisper.

"I don't care anymore." He'd leaned down and pressed his lips against hers. She kissed him back angry and hard. "I would lay down my life for you Cece. I would take the weight of it all to make you happy." She'd stared up at him, her eyes devouring his. He saw the moment she understood the depth of his love for her. Truly understood.

"We will do this together. We will, and we will be free when it ends."

That particular evening had been fiery and passionate. In sync, they had laid out all their desires and love and fused them together.

Matteo looked around the small home. Cece would hate it. It had no life, no flowers growing from the dirt. He'd yet to clean. He resolved to remedy that tomorrow. The least he could do was make this a place she would love when she finally joined him. Here, together, they would watch Gabriel's final decimation on the news before going home. Cocooned in this little cabin they would smile and toast and celebrate. Yes, he needed to make the house just right for Cece's return. Once their masterful illusion was complete she would need a home to return to, even if only temporarily.

Chapter 4

June 2014

~ Matteo ~

~***~

LYING IN WAIT; (1) a concealment of purpose, (2) a substantial period of watching and waiting for an opportune time to act, and (3) immediately thereafter, a surprise attack on an unsuspecting victim from a position of advantage[.]' "

~***~

"Fiore mio, I've missed you so," he said before scooping his wife into a bear hug. She squealed and squeezed him back tightly. "Tell me, how've you been? What's been going on?" he asked as he set his wife to her feet.

"There is so much to tell! Sit, sit!" A nasty smile of expectation crept across his face.

Matteo chuckled at her enthusiasm and sat. "She's let on that her parents are unhappy. So *very* unhappy. I can't even express how ridiculously happy it makes my heart to hear her speak. They're terrible Teo! They missed her graduation!"

Matteo stared in disbelief. "That can't be right. Why?"

"My God Teo, they are so wrapped up in their own stink that they've all but forgotten about Belle. It's almost as if she doesn't exist in their home. It's tragic really."

He shot her a pointed look. "Not too tragic I hope."

"Very funny stud. No it's perfect for me. She . . . she loves me I think. Like a . . . mother." He could tell the word stung her a bit. No doubt because she'd have given anything to have children of her own. It worried him, this bond she was forming with the girl. "I had Mark, the boy she likes, and that friend Madison help me out a little. I gave her a graduation party. You should have seen her eyes Teo. Such gratitude radiating from them. Such love. I swear, this entire situation couldn't have worked out any better. I'm just . . . over the moon about it all."

"Cece," he deadpanned.

"Don't Cece me," she cut in and wagged a

finger at him. " I haven't lost focus on the goal. I'm telling you all this because it feels . . . right. It's as if the last twenty years we've spent dreaming and scheming were leading up to this exact moment."

"I'm happy if you're happy," he answered.

She narrowed her eyes at him. "Cut the shit Teo, what's going on?"

"I'm . . ." he struggled to find the words he needed to say. He didn't want to sound weak. He prided himself on always being strong. For her, for them, for survival.

Celeste looked at him. Took him in for a long moment. "You're lonely." She tilted her head to the side. "You're feeling useless." He felt his brows lift. It had always fascinated him how she could do that. Read him so perfectly. As if they shared some portion of their DNA. He sighed.

"I miss bringing a plant home to you every day. Our walks, watching you in the garden. The ballroom dance lessons. I miss reading aloud together at night. I miss us, Cece." She stood then strode to him. She sat on his lap and he let his arms wrap around her waist.

"Oh Teo, this must be torture for you. I forget that you are out there alone while I'm in here surrounded by people. Never a dull moment you know. People rambling, fighting to find the right word that they can't remember to keep a conversation going. I'm so very selfish, although…you do have *real* food out there," she pointed out the window, "whereas I'm stuck eating preservative-ridden pre-packaged nastiness. So there's that."

Matteo laughed. Cece was very particular about the food she ate and this place did not live up to those expectations in the least. He could tell in the way her clothes were a little loser. She had lost just a touch of weight.

"Yes. You have been very selfish. Maybe you need to make it up to me." He grinned at her.

"You silly man, I plan on making it up to you for the rest of my life."

~***~

Matteo's visit buoyed his spirits. A lump of cheese dripped to the plate from his breakfast sandwich. Tossing the half-eaten sandwich on his plate he let out a massive sigh. Rain pelted the windows. Matteo missed home. One of their favorite things was to sit on their porch and listen to the rain come down. Revel in the thunderclaps and lightning bolts that lit up the sky. A deep roll of thunder that vibrated his bones made his thoughts scatter like spiders into the dark corners of his subconscious. The storm was almost here. In just twenty-four hours' time he would be mailing a letter meant to snap the final cord holding Gabriel and Monique together. He pulled a cigarette from his pocket. Lit it.

Inhaled.

Exhaled.

~***~

1998 - June

*M*y head spun, full of scenarios. My mind ticked over all the opportunities that I could take or leave, so I got up out of bed, dressed and started walking. There was no point in lying stagnant. When I took stock of my surroundings I found myself there. That sad place where so many died. The restaurant that serves no more patrons. I walked around and played things back in my head. It was eerily quiet except for the occasional outburst of chirping from the birds in the trees. The air felt so warm in my lungs. Emotions built, one upon the other and part of me just wanted to lie down there, among the ruins of that restaurant — let the building heat take me. I couldn't though. All life is interwoven, like fine silks in a tapestry. Darkness makes me aware of the stars. And when those dark hours emerge they still hold a bright and lovely thing. It is in my dreams that I am able to encounter what's departed my life and look at it. Converse with it. Alter the truth. Twist it and mold it until it suits me.

Gabriel injured my flesh, the skin and muscle. Memories make me strong. It's my hell. Shattered. Now I must take time to accept my dark reality. To kill the lights inside my soul and lose my identity. My hands are frigid yet my heart hot. It burns with ire. Logic has crushed my spirit. I have nothing to lose. I'm beautiful pain and ugly joy. I do nothing.

No, I'm lying in wait with nothing to do.

~***~

The time was long past for honest men, Matteo thought. Sweet dreams were made from these small moments. Summer swung wide now but the rains that sat on the horizon would wash away the pain of the past and set the two of them free.

Matteo grinned and kept reading.

~***~

2000 - Spain/Canada

*M*y dreams have taken a new shape. I am the evil lurking. I am the monster hiding in the closet, under the bed, the shadow that follows. Waiting. In my dreams Gabriel looks up at me, pale and grim, pleading. I take no pity. I offer him no mercy.

I carved Teo's and my initials in the dust with my

stiletto heel so someone would know we had been there. That we existed in beauty together. Healed here together. Loved here together. I had pins and needles anticipating what was to come. We're leaving our Spanish villa. It's time now.

We've located Gabriel.

Her face had been so close to his then that they would have touched noses had he turned his head. He let her read the email from the private investigator. She'd cut her eyes to his and smirked. She had looked so incredibly joyful. He couldn't resist. His lips found hers. Warmth had flooded him. Cece, his Cece, was so beautiful. So pure. And she was his. They were reckless renegades. A prelude to a shift. Together beginning a new chapter. It had been an exciting time.

Matteo closed the journal, content for the evening. He filled a watering can and watered the plants, all Cece's favorites, before turning in for the night.

In bed, Matteo pulled the covers up over him. He snatched the empty pillow beside him and clung to it as he drifted into dreams where the past and the future fought to the death.

Chapter 5

July 2014

~ *Matteo* ~

~***~

LYING IN WAIT — the act of concealing yourself and lying in wait to attack by surprise

~***~

Matteo sealed the letter in the envelope and kicked the trunk of the Volkswagen to quiet the man, not that it mattered. He stuck a stamp to the top left-hand corner then addressed it.

He drove for two hours until he reached a copse of trees far off any beaten path. After putting the car in park he ran a hand through his thick dark hair. He opened the door, swung his legs out and reached in his shirt pocket for a cigarette. He let the unlit smoke dangle between his lips before pushing up onto his feet.

He rounded the back of the car and popped the trunk open. The country club tennis instructor lay tied and squirming. Matteo pulled the syringe from his pocket, uncapped it and squirted a bit out the tip before bending over the man in the trunk and injecting the paralyzing drug into his system. Knowing the man wouldn't be moving or squealing would make it easier for him to dig the man's grave. He started shoveling.

Sweat dripped from his forehead and blisters had already formed on his palms. He took a break to enjoy a smoke. He didn't know what to feel really. Panic? No. Guilt? Only a little. This man was not part of Gabriel's family but he *did* serve a purpose. Matteo watched the way the hot breeze ruffled the leaves on the trees surrounding him. He tossed the shovel aside and looked over his work. Good enough. He hefted the man into his arms, stood and walked to the grave where he dropped the man in unceremoniously. There was no point in theatrics.

The man stared up at him wild-eyed. A pang of disgust filled Matteo. He didn't carry a gun. He absolutely wasn't going to smash the poor man's head in with a rock or other blunt object - it wasn't in him. He wasn't coldhearted. This was a means to an end. If there was a way to put him out of his mercy more humanely he would. But at present, there wasn't.

Sighing, he picked up the shovel and began tossing the dirt back into the ground being sure to cover the man's face first. It was unnerving having the man stare up at him. His was a senseless death, to anyone besides Matteo and Celeste. No one would understand it. It wouldn't be a moment of clarity for the man, he would just continue staring up at Matteo and wondering why. Matteo's heart raced. His blood thundered in his veins as he scooped dirt and tossed it in quickly. His work didn't take too take long and Matteo was pleased when he finally dropped the shovel into the trunk of the car. He turned and inspected the site. The ground hardly looked disturbed. Not that it mattered.

Hours.

It had taken hours of his day to complete his task. Matteo stopped at a mailbox and dropped the letter inside before stepping into the convenience store to grab something cold to cool him. By the time he arrived home that night he was bone tired and irritable. Cece had killed before, but she'd had him to come home to when she was a mess. He had no one waiting for him. No one to take the weight off his shoulders - not tonight anyways.

He kicked off his shoes and washed his hands repeatedly. The soil seemed to stain his skin. He wanted the reminder gone. He trudged through the kitchen and into the living room and let himself sink deep into the chair and relax. He reached for Cece's journal and laid it open in his lap, eager to read her words and imagine her voice. He needed her right now.

~***~

2002 - Canada

We took a trip, Teo and I, to the U.S., and from a very safe distance we watched Gabriel and Monique. My faith lies somewhere between lilies and pews. They have a secret life that they come home to every night. Matteo is outraged. How? he asks. It's as if karma doesn't exist. But I don't know, so I have no words for him.

I want to watch them fall. I want to hear the sound of the break, the sound of all the years they've saved up together snapping. Crackling in a fire. How it will burn. They will finally feel the fear, the humility of it all. Twenty years of a golden life of lies, melted down to nothing.

When we arrived back to our rental house we'd wracked our brains. We had so much more direction now that we'd seen them alive and well. We had all the time in the world to plan and execute the way we wanted. There were no limitations for us. Money and time are two things that every devil needs and we have it . . . so much of it.

~***~

The scars of her love left him breathless. Scars never leave. They stick around forever. Matteo was content knowing Cece had scarred him. It was something no one could take away. A scar couldn't be taken back. Their mutual hate, their wounds, their love was all consuming and it burned brighter than a comet. The promise that for Gabriel, death would not end his suffering made their bond that much stronger. He didn't need to die. He needed to suffer.

~***~

2004 - Canada

*W*e've had the most fun. America has so much to offer a traveler. There is so much to see. Matteo and I have been able to travel all over Canada and the U.S. and it has been bliss. We've met the most incredible people. Seen jaw-dropping sights and indulged in fabulous food. I feel like we are the two luckiest people. We have each other. We have the means to do whatever we'd like and we share the same mindset. We are so fortunate to be able to take advantage of all these experiences. At night when we're curled up in bed together, no matter where we are I get the strangest sense that everything has happened exactly the way it was meant to in my *life. That the lingering darkness that shrouds me still sometimes will explode into shards of light when we're done.*

When he's done. There is no greater suffering than losing everything. So we will not harm Gabriel, physically. We will strip him down bare until there is nothing left of him but his own ruined memories. And then leave him to live with it.

~***~

Matteo closed the journal and his eyes and thought back to their time in Canada. He loved that the happier she grew, the more she embraced her feelings, the shorter her entries became. They'd had friends in the neighborhood where they rented. It had been an exciting time for them. Potlucks and cookouts and festivals and game nights. There always seemed to be noise there. Alive. Writhing. Infecting them with all the world had to offer. Poisoning them with light. Everything in their journey did seem to have a time and place in hindsight. They had fallen into everything exactly when they had needed to.

~***~

Celeste stood at the window, feet set apart, hands shoved in her pockets, like it was Cece facing the world. Matteo didn't know what she was thinking; he was afraid to know. When she stood so still, like she did now, her mind was dangerous.

"Cece," he called. She turned to him. Her eyes, wide and vulnerable, flitted across his face, each of her breaths coming faster than the one before it. She licked her lips with the tip of her tongue and let out one long, slow blow that made him shudder.

"It's done."

He let the words hang out there like laundry drying in the wind. She walked toward him in even, measured strides. Using her fingertips, she followed his jawline, leaving a prickling trail behind. He wiped his thumb across her lower lip. Beyond thought, he leaned forward, lips parted hungrily. Her eyes darted between his mouth and eyes, gauging his expression, reading his desire. It was impossible to think about anything but her mouth on his, how she'd pull him into her arms and they'd burn together, forgetting about everything but the two of them. His body wanted it, his heart needed it, and it was clear hers did too.

They lay side by side in her bed afterwards enjoying their afterglow, reveling in the high of it.

"She is a fool for that boy Mark," Cece laughed. Delighted really. Her laughter, as always, sounded like the breeze tickling wind chimes. "Teo, my love, Monique left. Left the family! It worked. One sad suicide note to her and she crumbled. Finally. How was it? Hard?" Her voice dripped with honey, too sweet for good intentions. He grinned.

"Tedious, but not hard per se."

Cece snaked her arms around his waist. Lips kissed his bare chest.

"Was it very horrible going home afterward?"

"Without you there?" he asked. Cece nodded. "Yes. It left me alone with my thoughts fiore mio." She nodded again at him, understanding.

"I love you," she breathed.

"And I, you. Tell me, how are things going here?"

"Selfies," she muttered.

"What?"

"Those damn pictures you take of yourself. Selfies. She made me contort my face into utterly ridiculous positions and take pictures with her."

"Cece, what if she shows them to *him?*"

"Teo, you worry too much. What are the odds of a teenage girl sharing photos on her phone with her father?"

He shrugged. He didn't know a damned thing about teenage girls besides those whose pants he'd tried to get into decades ago.

"Did you bring the ring?" she asked changing the subject. A sure sign that she was nervous. He couldn't blame her, they were nearing the finale. A finale twenty years in the making. He lifted his pants from the floor and dug in the pocket until he caught the old engagement ring between his thumb and forefinger and lifted it out. "I did." It sparkled in the lamp light, the diamond still brilliant. He held it out to her but she remained still, staring at it as if it might grow teeth and bite her. "Cece," he murmured. Her eyes snapped to his. "It doesn't mean anything. It holds nothing over you." Wide-eyed she reached for it and let it sit in her palm.

"I don't want to look at it," she whispered. "It was a different life. String it on my necklace for me so I don't have to look at it."

Matteo leaned in and kissed her forehead. Cece sat upright. She sighed. He reached around and brushed her silky hair over one shoulder, exposing her graceful neck. Matteo placed a soft kiss to the bare spot before he unclasped the decades-old locket from her neck. She took one end from his hand and dropped the engagement ring onto the chain.

Matteo took the end she held and re-fastened the clasp. "You *are* the key, you know." His fingers grazed the sensitive skin at the nape of her neck and she shivered. "You are the key to me." Goosebumps broke out across her skin and he grinned. He let a finger trail her neckline.

"Teo," she breathed.

"What is it you want fiore mio?" He kissed the shell of her ear. Then just under it. Another kiss followed lower, then another. "Tell me," he urged.

"You Teo. Always you." It was all the invitation he needed as he laid his wife backwards onto the bed.

~***~

Matteo rode the high from his visit with Cece for the next week. They had lain in bed afterwards for hours talking. Dreaming. Living. Only a month to go and they would be reunited. No clouds lurking above their heads. Free and clear like the ocean tide rolling in and out. Sparkling and beckoning anyone willing to visit it. He'd gone to the dealership and purchased a candy apple red Porsche to pick her up in. Celeste loved convertibles. She laughed and smiled and said that the fresh air did wonders for the soul.

He spent his final days arranging the house just so. He stocked the cabinets with her favorites and made sure a live plant sat on every windowsill. The next time he'd see her would be the last time they'd have to steal mere hours together. Matteo dug the last of the drug out of the case in the closet and set it on the kitchen counter so he wouldn't forget it. It had been harder than they'd expected to get their hands on it but money seems to do miraculous things. Everyone has a price he'd learned.

Hopping into bed he let himself sink in the too soft mattress. Only five more weeks here and then they would go home. He missed their house. The smell of it. The ocean air, the freedom of the waves, their routine.

He cracked open the journal skipping ahead several entries. He didn't need her words to relive their happy times.

~***~

2005 - Trip to US

heir life looks so pretty. They are country clubbers. There are kids. Comfortable wealth. Monique and Gabriel have managed to make a sweet little life for themselves. Start anew. It repulses me. But it's evident in Gabriel's eyes, even from a watchful distance, that something is missing. That he mourns the loss of his esteemed position perhaps. That this new life isn't quite enough. If he only knew. It will never be enough. In fact, it will get worse-so much worse.

~***~

2005 - Us

We moved! It's a quaint town just five hours south of them. Matteo and I explored the area and simply fell in love. The ocean rushes and the salt hangs in the air. It's heaven. Two months ago we bought a house. It's ours and it's a dream. No more moving. No more renting. We've planted roots.

Teo brings me plants for the garden nearly every day. I spend most of my time creating something beautiful for us to enjoy year after year in the future. In the evenings we take quiet walks down the beach nearby. Hand in hand. The level of bliss that consumes me, devours me here, is overwhelming. Teo makes a fire in the pit out back most evenings and we drink and laugh and snuggle. On the nights it rains he picks up a random paperback from the bookcase and beckons me to lay with him as he reads it aloud. If this is a glimpse into our future we are going to be the happiest pair God ever created. We haven't lost sight of our goal but we've had a nice reprieve as of late to simply enjoy each other without anything looming over us. We have new papers. New names. We are Teo and Cece Grant. We've been Jezebel and Ahab for so long that we held onto those papers just in case we ever need to go back to Europe.

~***~

Matteo thought back to that time, to those names, and laughed. Jezebel and Ahab. Gabriel the king and Monique the harlot. It had seemed so funny then to pick those names. They had never used them together but on paper, that was who was married. In their hearts they would always be Cece and Teo. A familiar gnawing ache of separation spread through his chest. He thought about how they laughed together. She giggled at his puns but would get nearly hysterical at any type of potty humor. Some of their conversations could easily have come from a couple of ten-year-olds snickering at the lunch table. Matteo closed the journal then set it aside. He tucked his hands behind his head and wondered if Cece was sleeping now or lay awake thinking of him, as he did her.

He heard her scream. Then again. Gabriel's hands around her neck squeezed with vicious intent. The girl, Annabelle, stood grinning. The window separating him from Cece was thick-too thick. He pounded his fists on the glass but it didn't make a sound. No one looked his way. Cece's eyes strained in their sockets before drooping closed. He screamed.

Matteo bolted upright, sweat beaded on his forehead, the bed empty beside him. In his head, he drowned his fears until they disappeared and he found sleep again. Everything was fine.

~***~

He opened his eyes slowly. Let the light filter

in bit by bit until his eyes adjusted fully. Rolling to his side he grabbed the pack of cigarettes from the side table and his lighter and lit one up. She'd kill him for smoking in the bedroom but he still had time before she would be here to nag him about it. He was comfortable. He'd slept well after falling back asleep which was a surprise. Feeling lazy he reached for her journal and spread it open next to him on the bed. He'd read just a little more before getting up.

~***~

2006 - Us

*B*rant is dead. I feel guilty, but not guilty enough. I was sitting in the car watching him. My body stiff, hyper-aware of the noise and the daylight and fear of discovery. He looked just like a young Gabriel. Handsome. My heart swelled then burst. The fury that sprouted inside my soul overcame me. I slammed the gas pedal down and closed my eyes. I killed him.

A boy.

Gabriel's boy.

Monique's boy.

I had to bite back the tears that came, hot and fast. My stomach turned in half delight, half overwhelming sickness at my action. I didn't look. I sped away. Called Matteo.

I barely made it to our hotel before I had an attack. I barely had time to shout his name into my phone from the parking lot. Vomit covered me in the driver's seat. Sweat dripped from my forehead. My hair stuck to my neck uncomfortably. My knuckles white from fisting them against the cramping and pain. Matteo swept me up. Carried me. Hydrated me. Placated me. He held me together while I couldn't do it for myself. He did not get angry that it had happened without him. He did not scold me for not sticking to our plan.

The next night Matteo kissed the tip of my hip bone. A shudder ran through me. Delight. Desire. Joy. Magic. His love so endless that it brought tears to my eyes. We made love. Celebrated another milestone in our quest. Our mission. It united us further, if possible.

He will dream with me at night as we grow old together. The pain, the guilt of what I've done vanished, faded away. And when we woke in the morning, he disposed of the car for me.

~***~

He should have had his coffee first. Matteo tried not to get caught up in that particular entry but it brought many memories back. Sleepless nights spent cooing Cece back to sleep. It was too late to quit then and they both had known it. Cece had deviated from their plan and in a rush of emotion she'd taken a step she couldn't take back and the only option left was moving forward-so they had. It had irked him then. He was a planner. He needed the feeling of control that having set guidelines gave him. But Cece had struggled with what she'd done and he knew he had to abandon the irritation he felt and just deal with what was.

They'd followed and watched the Fortin family for months. By observing, things slowly snapped into place for them. The tennis instructor sleeping with Monique stuck out as an easy target. If they removed him from the situation it would break her. Monique's dull eyes perked right up each time she was with the man. The girl would be the real kicker but Monique was another nail in Gabriel's coffin and quite frankly, Matteo wanted Gabriel to feel the complete loss of a marriage he actually *chose*.

He would never be able to look at Monique the same way when she came clean. Even in their rare grieving together Monique would no longer be a source of comfort for Gabriel. Not this time. This would break the last ties they shared.

Chapter 6

August 2014

~ Matteo ~

~***~

LYING IN WAIT – *waiting in concealment; in ambush.*

~***~

As he sauntered down the hallway he thought of his wife's late night call a week ago.

"I can't sleep," was her way of greeting him. He'd smiled feeling important. "Close your eyes. Think about the waves, hear them crashing on the sand, the sweet smell of flowers and sea spray mixing together and surrounding you, and the cool night air on your skin as our bedroom curtains blow in the breeze. Feel my arms around you. Holding you tight. Think about me and how during summer thunderstorms we would sit on our deck under the awning watching the rain *fall." She'd sighed. He swore he could hear the smile playing on her lips. "Sleep fiore mio." She mumbled she loved him and he stayed on the line until her breaths were an even, deep rhythm.*

This was the end.

His last visit to her.

All day he had been bored, distracted, annoyed.

"I almost *died* Teo. She looked me up." His wife's words were lost on him at present. He was fixated on the glint coming from her nose. His wife had pierced her nose?

"Are you even listening to me?!"

He blinked. Then laughed. Loud and hard. What had she done? "Teo!" she yelled.

He cupped her face between his hands. "I'm sorry, but what exactly is this?" He let the tip of his finger graze the fresh piercing. Cece's eyes bulged and her hand flew up to her nose.

"Well shit. I forgot!" She cackled with laughter. "That damn girl. She snuck me out. Made me do it! It was this or a tattoo. I think I chose wisely. Don't you like it?" She laughed more. He loved her laugh. She sounded lighter today. The anticipation of her last visit with the girl was surely a turn on.

"It's new, that's for sure," he chuckled low.

"Anything else I should know about?" he asked and spun her around to inspect her.

Cece giggled. "Hmm, let's see, Gabriel is diligently trying to repair his relationship with his daughter. Clinging to his one last shred of hope. Belle's in love and all that we need is the vial. Her last visit is only a week away."

"I have it," he answered smirking. "Are you sure you're ready? You can do this?"

"I've never been more ready. I want to come home Teo. I want my life back."

Matteo pointed to the bag he'd set on the side table when he'd entered. "Everything is in there. Use the entire vial." Celeste walked to the bag, opened it and retrieved the small glass vial. She held it up to the light inspecting it.

"It looks like water you know? So deceptive. So insidious," she commented with a smile playing on her lips. Matteo nodded in agreement. It did. It was also perfect for their needs in more than one way.

"Come here." He watched his wife obediently obey. "The next time I see you, you will be a different woman."

"Kiss me Teo, kiss me one last time in this dark shadow we live in so that the next time our lips meet, it will be in truth," she said. He kissed her. "In light." He kissed her again more deeply. She pulled back and looked up at him. "What if the light is boring? What if we want to let the shadows in now and again?" she asked wide-eyed, as if just realizing that their life wouldn't be tied to a goal after Tuesday.

Teo smiled.

"Then we let the shadows creep in when they need to." Cece bit her lip and held his eyes. He thumbed her lip away from her teeth and gently bit the pouty lower one. "We'll be anything you need," he assured her. She pushed him then, causing him to collapse in the chair behind him. She straddled his lap, running both hands through his hair, and gently pulled backward until his throat was exposed to her. He swallowed loudly, keeping the moan that threatened to escape from doing so, wanting to tease her into thinking he wasn't as affected as he was but needing her touch more than anything. They kissed one another with the kind of passion that only comes once in a lifetime. Soft lips pressed to the hollow of his throat and he moaned low and raw. He kissed her mouth and ran his nose up along her cheek, burrowing into her hair. As need ratcheted higher, he secured his arms around her and stood before carrying her to the bed, shadows all around them, hungry and carnivorous.

~***~

Matteo woke with a smile on his face. In five

short days he would be on his way to pick up his wife. He thought of their weakest moments, their strength that kept them stable and inspired to push on. The way neither was immune to pain or frustration, but handled it well, and knew how to pull themselves up from low places. The way they never missed a call from one other, always willing to be there for each other. Loyalty, devotion, and a true pillar in each other's worlds. He thought about how when the world around her crumbled and the sun seemed as if it would never rise again, his love still believed—his faith in her his foundation.

Their love was unlike others.

It got them through the good and the bad, and it never faltered. When the world turned cold, hope, morals, kindness, and goodwill gone, they lifted each other up. And now, they were to face a new chapter in their lives. An unknown. Free of guilt and shame and betrayal. The idea scared him as much as it excited him. In five days they would take that first step together, again, into unknown waters. His faith in them didn't waver; he knew as sure as his heart beat in his chest that they would find their way and be happy.

He snagged her journal from the bedside table and flipped toward the end with a smile on his face.

~***~

2008 - USA

*I*t's all about perception. Life. My life is so full now. Bursting at the seams. We lie on the beach and stare at the stars at night. We make up stories for each one. Teo's stories are so much better than mine. His imagination endless. One of the things I adore about him the most. His words, his stories, his heartbeat all seep into my soul and lift me higher than I thought possible. The small gestures and touches. His hand on my rear, pulling me against him. He seems to prefer me that way, tightly tucked up against his side. I don't think I will ever get used to someone needing to touch me so much. Although, I share the same sentiment. My hands don't like to leave his. My lips hate not touching his skin, tasting it. The smell of him alone is a comfort. My Teo is so much more than a partner, a husband, a friend. He's the blood in my veins. He is gravity. He is the air in my lungs. They don't have a word for that kind of person, that kind of union. It's a shame. It would be a beautiful word.

~***~

2012 - USA

We've been spying. It's rather fun. We make up stories as we watch each of them go about their days. How tired Monique looks. How she's having an affair with the tennis instructor at the country club. How Gabriel is a workaholic who strangely spends no time with his family — the one thing he seemed to so desperately want. Okay, so maybe they aren't lies so much as truths. But Teo and I have great fun embellishing the little details that we're privy too. They go about their lives unaware of our presence. It's a strange thing to be a voyeur. It's a strange sensation to know that you are playing God. And we are — aren't we? Watching and learning their lives piece by piece so that we can alter them, manipulate them. The joy that embraces me is overwhelming.

~***~

The last entry in the journal is one he'd not read before. He'd saved it. Savored the very idea of it, for conclusion, for this moment. In just thirty minutes he'd leave to pick up his wife. He scanned the small home, making sure everything was just as he wanted it. Mentally confirming that everything was perfect for their return, he grabbed the book and flipped the journal open to the end. She'd run out of blank pages long ago and instead of letting him buy her a new journal she'd simply written on loose paper and stuffed them into the back. This last entry was special. It was a day that seemed to have been laid at their feet on a plate of gold and he found himself dizzy with excitement to read Cece's perception of it.

~***~

2014 - March

The courtroom was small. It made me nervous sitting so near to the girl and Monique. It's funny that with years passed by lifetimes can be forgotten. Monique walked right by me without thinking twice. I'm a ghost in her world. Long forgotten. The judge handed out no leniency. Sentenced the girl to six months' probation volunteering at a center for patients with early onset dementia. She starts in two weeks. When I left the courtroom, I felt buoyant. Joyous.

Matteo and I used a good chunk of money to buy my way into Glenview. To buy the necessary doctor's recommendations quickly. Our old private investigator still useful all these years later. It was only sheer luck that Glenview even had space available. Maybe not luck but karma. As if my need for revenge, that deep-rooted and bloomed fury, my own personal religion, was watching out for me. For Matteo. All the cruel and ruthless disappointments mean nothing now. You earn your own luck and Matteo and I have definitely earned ours.

Tomorrow Matteo moves me into Glenview. Room 208. I'm excited and nervous. This closure, two decades in the making, is so close to completion now. That Matteo and I are so close to a life outside of this is a driving force deep within me. I'm so ready.

They say the morning after a storm brings the most incredible beauty. That the sky produces the most magnificent colors. That the air is still and calm. That you could sit for hours after watching the sunrise and feel the most spectacular sense of peacefulness.

They lie.

The morning after a storm simply means another one is lying in wait.

~***~

Matteo grinned at the written words. How perfectly well stated. Someday Cece would write a book about her life and what a book it would be. Matteo could almost smell the salt breeze from the ocean of home as anticipation and excitement raced through his veins. The precipice was upon him and he was willingly jumping off the dark edge toward the clear, green water below.

Six months felt like an eternity, but they had weathered it and now it was time to fire up the shiny red Porsche and pick up his wife. He could hardly contain his excitement. This was a new chapter and he was looking forward to it immensely. He knew she would be panicking right now even though he was just a few minutes behind. It was six thirty p.m.

He should be there already.

He pulled into the lot at breakneck speed, stopping once he reached the curb. A grin spread across Cece's face at the sight of him. He exhaled heavily. She was stunning. Grace and class neatly packaged, simply waiting for him to unwrap her. A gift. Cece was and had always been a gift in his life.

His wife.

She was his rock. His truth. His everything. He smiled, cigarette dangling from the corner of his mouth. She smiled back. Leaning over as she approached the car, he pushed the door open from the inside for her.

"*Fiorc mio,*" he cooed, admiring her sleek form.

"I missed you," she breathed. His lips found hers. Warmth flooded him. She was so incredibly stunning. So pure. Her love, her commitment, saved them both and now they could be truly free.

"Sei pronta?" he asked. Celeste twined their fingers together and rested their connected hands on her thigh before sighing contentedly. *It's over,* he thought.

Matteo put the car in drive and peeled out from the lot as people begin to rush out the doors frantically. The fire alarm blared in the distance. He throttled the gas and Cece squealed in delight. Her wide smile lit up his heart. Their past floated away until it was just a memory of a nightmare from the night before, leaving a new life in its wake. He couldn't suppress the laugh that bubbled up from his gut and fell out of his mouth as she squeaked again with joy, hair blowing wildly in the wind. Their sins blew away as they drove.

She was his and his only. Tonight they would celebrate and tomorrow they would make popcorn and tune into the news, watch the aftermath unfold and revel in it.

Together.

Free.

The End

Acknowledgments

To my readers. It is YOU who carry me along. YOU who motivate me to continue writing. My biggest thanks goes out to you, the reader, for taking a chance on me. For allowing me to slip into your life and steal your time. It's an honor. Thank you.

Want more of K. Larsen's work? Check out the <u>website</u>.

Want more of
K. Larsen's work?

30 Days ~ FREE

Committed

Bloodlines Series—All can be read as stand-alone books.

Tug of War ~ FREE

Objective

Resistance

Target 84

Stand Alones

Dating Delaney

Saving Caroline

Jezebel

About K. Larsen

K. Larsen is an avid reader, coffee drinker, and chocolate eater who loves writing romantic suspense and thrillers. If *you* love suspense and romance on top of a good plot you've hit the mother-load. She may mess with your head a bit in the process but that's to be expected. She has a weird addiction to goat cheese and chocolate martinis, not together though. She adores her dog. He is the most awesome snuggledoo in the history of dogs.

Seriously.

She detests dirty dishes. She loves sarcasm and funny people and should probably be running right now . . . because of the goat cheese . . . and stuff. Sign up for a chance to win a $5 Gift card every time she sends a newsletter out.

Stalk her — legally

Newsletter –
http://klarsenauthor.com/5-gift-card/

Amazon –
http://www.amazon.com/K.-Larsen/e/B00AN1BSIE

Goodreads -
http://www.goodreads.com/author/show/6871141.K_Larsen

Facebook -
https://www.facebook.com/K.LarsenAuthor

Twitter –
@Klarsen_author

Made in the USA
Middletown, DE
05 December 2022